To Peter Wesley, the newest McKissack   —P. C. M.

In thanksgiving for my talented granddaughters, Troi Nicole and Rene Gabrielle   —O. J. M.

For Catherine, Ian, and Delphine, with love   —K. B.

Atheneum Books for Young Readers
An imprint of Simon & Schuster
Children's Publishing Division
1230 Avenue of the Americas
New York, New York 10020
Text copyright © 2005
by Patricia McKissack and
Onawumi Jean Moss
Illustrations copyright © 2005
by Kyrsten Brooker
All rights reserved, including the right of
reproduction in whole or in part in any form.
Book design by Lee Wade and Jessica Sonkin
The text for this book is set in Minion.
The illustrations for this book are rendered in
collage and oil paints.
Manufactured in China
First Edition
1 2 3 4 5 6 7 8 9 10

Library of Congress Cataloging-in-
Publication Data
McKissack, Pat, 1944-
Precious and the Boo Hag / Patricia C. McKissack
and Onawumi Jean Moss ; illustrated by Kyrsten
Brooker.   p. cm.
"An Anne Schwartz Book."
Summary: Home alone with a stomachache while the
family works in the fields, a young girl faces up to the
horrifying Boo Hag that her brother warned her
about.
ISBN 0-689-85194-4
[1. Monsters—Fiction. 2. Courage—Fiction.
3. Sick—Fiction. 4. African Americans—Fiction.]
I. Moss, Onawumi Jean. II. Brooker, Kyrsten, ill.
III. Title.
PZ7.M478693 Lk 2004
[Fic]—dc21
2002001571

Precious
and the Boo Hag

Patricia C. McKissack
and **Onawumi Jean Moss**

Illustrated by
Kyrsten Brooker

AN ANNE SCHWARTZ BOOK
Atheneum Books for Young Readers
New York London Toronto Sydney

"Oooo-Wee!"

Precious had been up all night with a stomachache. Since it was corn planting time, every hand was needed in the fields. "Got no choice but to leave you here," Mama said. "Now remember, don't let nothing and nobody in this house—not even me, 'cause I got a key." After plenty of hugs and dozens of dos and don'ts, Mama finally left. "We're no farther than a stone's throw away," she called over her shoulder. "You need us, come a-running. Understand?"

"Yes, ma'am," Precious answered, feeling like a big girl. "Don't worry. I'll be fine."

Do your chores.

Do get yo' stuff off the floor.

Don't make a mess.

Don't ramble in my things.

Before he left, Brother pulled Precious to the side. "Be sure to mind Mama, now. 'Cause if you let somebody in, you never know. It just might be Pruella the Boo Hag."

"Who?" Precious asked, with a disbelieving giggle.

Brother scrunched his face. "Boo Hags live all over, everywhere, but Pruella is one who lives on the prairie. She's tricky and she's scary, and she tries to make you disobey yo' mama."

Precious held her breath as Brother went on. "Pruella is strange from head to toe. She aine too smart, got no manners, hates clean water, can change her shape, and tells whoppers." Then his voice lowered as he added, "And she'll do most *anything* to get inside."

"Wh-wh-why does she want to get inside?" Precious asked, her voice quavering.

Brother clicked his teeth. "You don't want to know. Just remember this: No Boo Hag can get inside your house, less'n you let her in." Then he rushed to catch up with Mama.

Now Precious was all by herself. She stood stone-still, listening to the quiet, hoping that if Pruella the Boo Hag was nearby, she wouldn't notice her . . . or see that she was alone.

"What you doin' standing like a bump on a pickle?" Addie Louise Patterson's voice boomed through the kitchen window, almost turning Precious inside out. "How come you not helping with the planting?"

"Got a stomachache," Precious answered. "And I can't let nothing and nobody inside, 'cause"—and she sighed deeply—"it might be Pruella the Boo Hag."

Addie Louise burst out laughing. "Who told you that silly ol' stuff? Aine no such thing as a Boo Hag."

"Really?" Precious said, mad that she'd fallen for another one of Brother's stories.

"Better watch out for the little green men from Mars, too," Addie Louise teased, and skipped away.

Even though Addie Louise was sure to tell the whole county that Precious was a scaredy-cat, the girl felt much better. "There's no such thing as a Boo Hag—especially one named Pruella," she told herself with a pinch of confidence.

To pass the time, Precious looked through Mama's handkerchiefs, then tried on her Sunday hat and high-heel shoes. She was having fun counting all the strawberry preserves, when suddenly the birds stopped singing. The air fell thick and cold. Honeysuckle wilted on the vine. And the sunny day took on a dark and dreary disposition.

Precious looked out the kitchen window. Didn't see nothing. She peered out the side windows. Didn't see nothing neither. But when she went to the front window, there it was, riding on the back of a storm—the biggest, meanest something Precious had ever seen. It had eyes of burning cinder and hair that shot out like lightning. "Pruella the Boo Hag is real," she whispered. "And she is one awful sight."

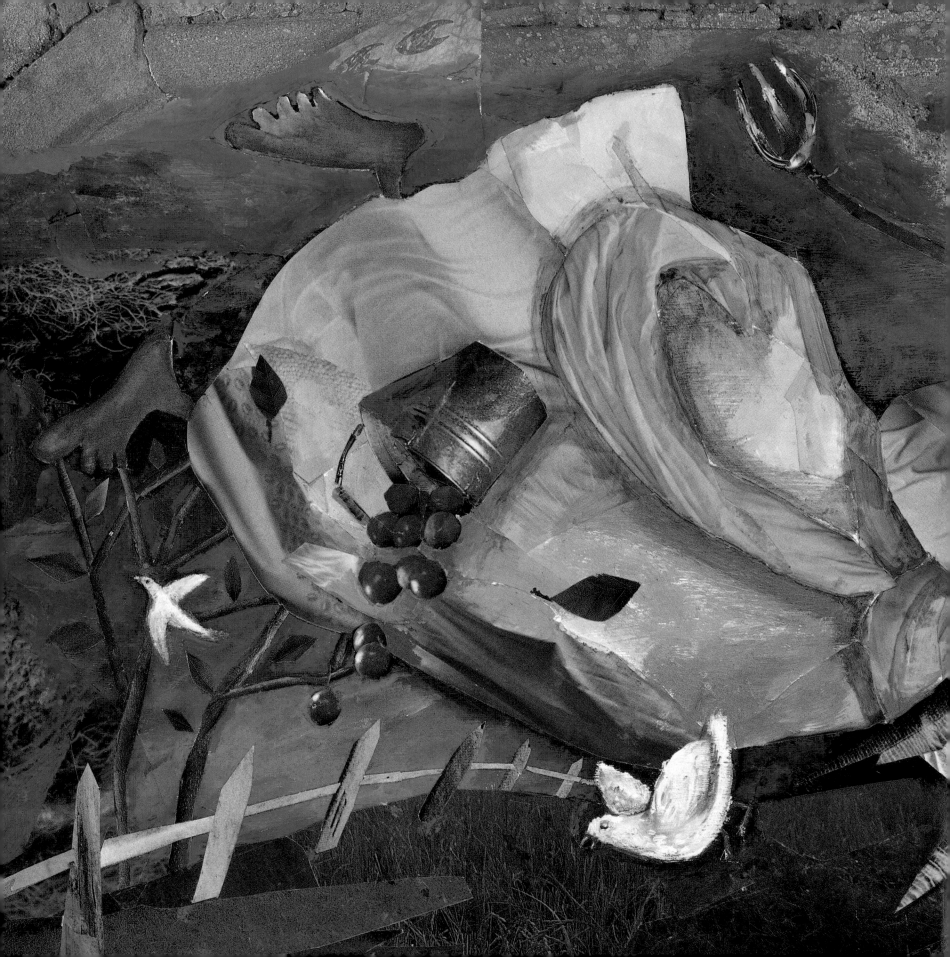

"Open the door and let me in!" shouted a voice that rumbled like rolling thunder. The wind whirled and twirled and shook the whole house.

Precious shook too, and in a small voice she answered, "My mama told me not to open the door for nothing and nobody." Quick, she dashed behind a curtain and sang her fear:

Pruella is a Boo Hag—
she's right outside my window.
She's tricky and she's scary,
but I won't let her in!

The Boo Hag howled and threw lightning. But Precious held fast. Louder and louder she sang, *"But I won't let her in!"*

At last Pruella grumbled and sputtered and—*poof!*—she was gone. Instantly the sun came out. The birds started chirping, and the daisies lifted their faces to the light.

Precious opened the front window and filled her lungs with fresh-smelling air. And she sang her victory:

Pruella is a Boo Hag —
she was right outside my window.
She's tricky and she's scary,
but I didn't let her in!

While she was still humming, a woman opened the front gate and came steppin' down the walk, looking like a runaway rainbow. "Morning to you," she spoke, real cheery, then took a seat in Mama's porch rocker.

"Good morning," Precious spoke back, noticing that the woman wore one pink shoe and one orange shoe.

"It's hot as you please," the visitor screeched, looking over Precious's head to see inside. "Bring me somethin' to drink—tea, juice, dirty dishwater will do."

"Did you say *dish*water?"

"Said no such thing," the woman snapped back. "Hurry up, anyhow. I'm thirsty."

Precious wondered if the strange woman had ever heard of please. Returning from the kitchen, she handed the woman a cup of water.

The woman flashed a crooked smile. "Now, young'un, let me inside to drink it in the cool."

Precious shook her head and backed away. "I'm not to let nothing and nobody in this house."

"Humph!" The woman grumbled and hissed and took a big gulp. "Water!" She gagged and coughed and sputtered. One eye went to spinning like a top, the other started blinking, and her tongue rolled out like a scroll. "I said tea, juice—anything," she gasped, "but never, never did I ask for clean, clear water!"

True to Brother's word, the visitor was strange from head to toe, had no manners, and hated clean water. "Can't trick me! I know who you are!" Precious said, and she slammed the window shut.

Outside, the woman grew taller and wider. She roared like a hundred swamp things, "Let me in!"

Precious sang to muster her courage:

With the melody swirling around her, the Boo Hag vanished.

Just then, Addie Louise came skipping up from around the side of the house. "Hello, Precious," she spoke, not sounding a bit like Addie Louise. *It looks like her, it walks like her, but it sure don't talk like her,* thought Precious, checking to see if Addie Louise's shoes and eyes matched.

"Got some jacks and a ball," said the girl, her voice all scratchy. "If you let me in, we can play."

"I told you, I'm not allowed."

Addie Louise smiled. Her teeth didn't look like hers either. "Yo' mama told me I could play inside with you."

Precious put her hand on the doorknob. "Well, if Mama says it's okay . . ."

The Addie Louise–thing got so excited her toes popped through her shoes. They were big and hairy and smelled awful.

Precious pulled back her hand. Thinking fast, she asked all sweetly, "Doesn't Mama look pretty today in her blue apron?"

"Umm-huh! Truly she does."

"You're telling a big whopper!" Precious shouted. "Mama's apron is green!"

Pruella is a Boo Hag—
she's right outside my window.
She's tricky and she's scary,
but I didn't let her in!

In a fit of fury the Boo Hag left, leaping wildly over the prairie like a March hare.

For the rest of the day Precious watched and waited for signs of Pruella the Boo Hag. As a late afternoon sunbeam struck the front porch, an orangish flash of light caught her eye. It was a penny, all sparkling new.

Precious wanted it. She tried to lean out the window to reach the coin, but it was too far away. She fetched the broom, but the penny wouldn't move. She'd have to go get it. Her stomach started hurting once more, and now her head ached too.

Slowly Precious opened the front door. Her eyes searched the yard—first right, then left. No sign of Pruella. In a dash she hurried out, snatched up the coin, and turned to go back inside. But on the threshold she stopped to look down at it. "No," she decided. "You can't fool me." And she flicked it over her shoulder. *Poof!* It was gone before it hit the ground.

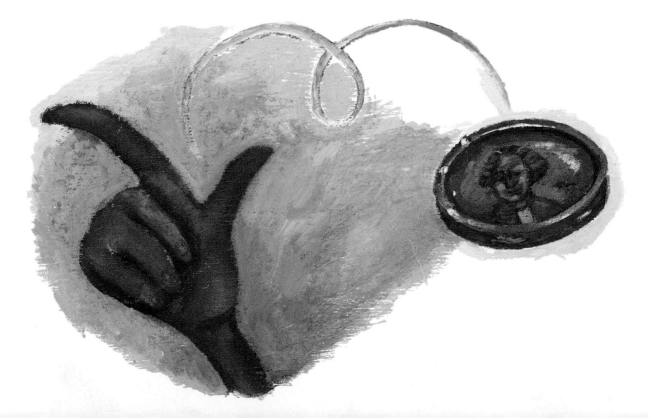

When Mama came home, she was very proud of Precious. "I knew I could trust you," she said, and gave her daughter a hug.

Later Precious told Brother everything that had happened. "Pruella was scary, and she was pretty tricky. I almost brought her inside when she disguised herself as a shiny new penny." She finished with a big smile. "But like you told me, a Boo Hag aine none too smart. George Washington was on the front instead of Abraham Lincoln."

That night Precious climbed into bed and drifted off to sleep, humming her victory song:

Pruella is a Boo Hag—
she was right outside my window.
She's tricky and she's scary,
but I didn't let her in!

As you listen to her gentle breathing, look closely in the branches outside Precious's window.

You may just see a strange and scary creature . . . waiting to get in!